T0132044

T.E. Corner

Balboa Press books may be ordered through booksellers or by contacting:

Balboa Press
A Division of Hay House
1663 Liberty Drive
Bloomington, IN 47403
www.balboapress.com
844-682-1282

Because of the dynamic nature of the Internet, any web addresses or links contained in this book may have changed since publication and may no longer be valid. The views expressed in this work are solely those of the author and do not necessarily reflect the views of the publisher, and the publisher hereby disclaims any responsibility for them.

Any people depicted in stock imagery provided by Getty Images are models, and such images are being used for illustrative purposes only. Certain stock imagery © Getty Images.

ISBN: 979-8-7652-3247-7 (sc)
ISBN: 979-8-7652-3248-4 (e)

Library of Congress Control Number: 2022914210

Print information available on the last page.

Balboa Press rev. date: 08/15/2022

BALBOA.PRESS

In honor of Antoine Béchamp.
Dedicated to Dr. Robert O. Young.
Love and Light.

Kylie is a wonderful girl,
she is happy and awake in this wonderful world.

Her parents taught her that true strength comes from deep down inside.
Her teachers, coaches, doctors and even her parents are simply a guide.

Does this sound strange to be so resilient with such a strong belief?
When we have this inner strength, nothing ever goes wrong which is such a relief.

Sure, people may doubt and disagree.
But belief like this does not need a college degree.

She gets it from her mother, this strength and never give-up attitude.
And she never forgets to express her gratitude.

Ever since her mother was diagnosed with stage four cancer,
she was determined to survive and find the real answer.

Going through treatments made her mom very sick, nauseous and weak.
It was so painful, making every day seem very bleak.

She wanted to know why the treatment for this disease
made people so sick and brought them to their knees.

The treatment got rid of the cancer for sure.
But she wanted to understand why it made her even sicker than before.

She was determined to make it through the pain and suffering,
to find the real cure even the experts were not offering.

Most people disagreed, ridiculing her and filling her with doubt.
Even family members did not understand what it was all about.

Despite these setbacks, criticism and attacks, her mother never backed down.
She remained determined to find the real cure, it was astonishing what she found.

Humans are silly, that they would rather be right and prove someone wrong,
instead of being at peace and accepting the truth all along.

Believe it or not, cancer treatments are not the cure.
Sure, it destroys the disease, but it wreaks havoc and so much more.

Her mother studied nutrition and how the body heals.
Then she met an amazing doctor who had even greater things to reveal!

The immune system is what keeps us healthy and feeling fine.
It's not anything new and has been the cure time after time.

It always has been and always will,
never coming in the form of an injection or a pill.

At least the way they are prescribed today.
Maybe people will wake-up someday to do it the right way.

And when they do, so many people will heal.
You will see miracles all over the world and, yes, this is for real!

By analyzing her blood, it was like looking at the rings of a tree.
She saw what happened in the past and what would come to be.

His words were simple, "All you need to do is change your lifestyle."
It was the greatest thing she heard in a long while.

The root of disease comes from what you drink, think, eat and breathe.
Changing her lifestyle was a simple approach and very easy to see.

You see, it is not a germ floating through the air that makes us ill.
And even if it were, the cure is not with a shot or a pill.

To cleanse from all this awful stuff,
the immune system expresses symptoms, interestingly enough.

We get a cough, sniffles, a fever or even worse,
all because these toxic and poisonous things are really a curse.

The idea of treating disease with disease, seemed strange to Kylie.
But her newfound knowledge about health and healing was the way to be.

When your blood and interstitial fluid are alkaline,
you have little to worry about and will always feel fine.

It's easy to fear and blame a germ or a silly virus for getting sick.
But when you awaken to real healing, it is cleansing the immune system that always does the trick.

Kylie chuckles when her friends hide at the sound of a cough or sneeze,
as if they were spreading a deadly disease.

Germs are a natural part of life,
and should not cause any strife.

PREVENTS DISEASE BODILY FLUID LONGEVITY
FOOD DIET
RAW FOODS
ABETES ALKALINE
ERTENSION
BONE DENSITY STROKE
RONIC PAIN
FRESH FRUITS ARTHRITIS
ORGANIC PH BALANCE ACIDITY AUTOIMMUNE
MUSCLE MASS
ALKALINE-PROMOTING ORGAN HEALTH
GREEN DRINKS

18

"Not afraid of germs! How could this be?" You might gasp.
This theory about germs was something Kylie believed, long ago in the past.

Once she learned about the healing power of the terrain,
her understanding of sickness was forever changed.

An alkaline immune system is the cure.
It is a simple as that and nothing more.

We do not get sick because of a germ.
We have had it backwards all along and still have a lot more to learn.

Changing her lifestyle wasn't easy for her mother to do.
But now her mother no longer gets sick, not even the flu.

At Kylie's school, her teacher said, "Wash your hands, you know its flu season."
Because her teacher believed a virus was the reason.

After her mother's crusade and newfound knowledge,
Kylie knew a great deal about the immune system, more than what is taught in college.

Kylie chuckled at the comment and said with a smirk,
"No, no. That's not how it works."

"What did you say?"
Her teacher replied in dismay.

"Believing we get sick because of germ or virus floating in the air is pretty lame."
Kylie continued, "We get sick because we don't take care of our terrain."

22

"Yes, we are indoors more because of shorter days and less sunlight.
We spend time with friends and family during the holidays feeling merry and bright.

"Eating more candy, processed foods and junk,
just poisons our immune system putting it into a funk.

"Our body shows symptoms and signs that we are sick, and we want to know why?
The reason we get the flu is because our immune system is trying to detoxify.

"A virus is not the culprit for the flu.
On the contrary it is a result of all the damage we do.

"It all starts in October with a little trick or treat.
Then comes Thanksgiving with drink, candy, pies and a bunch of turkey and ham to eat.

"Christmas comes with more junk and surprises.
The days are shorter. There's less daylight for sports and our favorite exercises.

"Our body gets very little sunlight or time for recreation,
diminishing its ability for circulation and respiration.

"We become stagnant and lazy.
This is when our immune system starts to go crazy.

"It needs to find a way to get the junk to pass through.
So, a fever, sniffles, chills, and body aches ensue.

"When we no longer pollute our terrain with this awful food, junk and injections,
is like coming back from the dead, a sort of resurrection."

Kylie saw her aunts, uncles, teachers, cousins and friends injecting poison into their arms.
Seemingly with very little regard for the potential of long-term damage and harm.

This made her worry and wonder why they would do such a thing.
Did they ever ask what it truly was and what harm it would bring?

Despite dozens of jabs over the years and people still getting sick,
did anyone ever ask why these jabs and injections rarely did the trick?

When Kylie was a baby, she was at the doctor's office for an annual visit,
Her mother asked the doctor, "What's in it?"

"What are the ingredients of this thing you are going to inject into my child?"
The doctor paused and her demeanor change from mild to wild.

The doctor was caught off guard by such a simple question.
And then replied with a bit of aggression.

"Do you want it or not!" The doctor firmly stated.
"No, I don't," said Kylie's mom. "And why are you so agitated?"

The doctor demanded, "You must take the shot!"
Kylie's mother replied, "What if I do not?"

"Why are you acting this way?" She continued.
"It's my choice and I have a say."

The doctor demanded, "No you don't and you're going against my advice."
"Thank you," Kylie's mom replied. "I've made up my mind and don't need to think twice."

Although the doctor was clearly disagreeing,
Kylie's mother was looking out for her well-being.

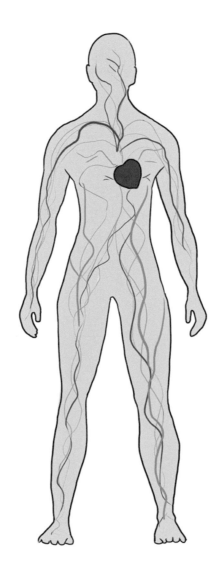

Sure, it seemed like a harmless little jab in Kylie's arm,
but her mother wanted to make sure this would not cause any long-term harm.

Kylie is glad her mother stood strong.
Because she now understands that we have been wrong all along.

Germs do not make us sick,
On the contrary, it is because of so many things that are toxic.

Bad food, bad water, dirty air, bad thoughts and medications are to blame.
And the true way to heal is to reclaim our terrain.

We all have a superpower that most of us neglect.
It's so easy to take for granted and allow it to go unchecked.

Just like kryptonite drains Superman of his powers.
Bad food, water, air, thoughts and medications make our immune system cower.

When we fill our body with junk,
the natural result is to go into a funk.

We continue to bombard our bodies with awful stuff and rubbish.
Our superpower begins to weaken, and we feel sluggish.

When we show symptoms, like a runny nose or cough,
they are just signs that something is off.

Symptoms are expressions and signs.
And our immune system is telling us something is wrong inside.

When we try to heal and cure disease with disease.
This only makes things worse, bringing our immune system to its knees.

ANTOINE BÉCHAMP

"Treat the patient,
not the infection."

Dis-ease is from
a Weakened
Immune System

GERM THEORY

TERRAIN THEORY

VACCINATE THE FISH

CLEAN THE TANK

Maybe you wonder what you should do.
And if any of this is this really true.

Pills, injections and drugs do not cure.
They are just a temporary solution that keep you coming back for more.

You see, we are customers for life.
And revealing the cure would cause a lot of strife.

For example, when a goldfish is sick,
what typically does the trick?

Do you treat the fish or change the water?
It's a simple answer, just ask your son or daughter.

Kylie doesn't get sick or take any medications.
Sure, she is like any other kid and eats lousy food, candy and other enjoyable libations.

When her terrain is out of balance, sniffles and a cough are often the sign.
This is when Kylie takes the right steps for her immune system to realign.

Kylie is not one to gab,
but she is proud that she has never gotten a jab.

Have you ever wondered why we are allergic to so many foods?
Or, why we see so many children with learning disabilities and strange moods?

The culprits are the toxic things you inject and ingest.
When you stop poisoning your body this will serve you best.

She believes in the healing power of Love.
Love is her strength, and nothing is above.

She hopes others will eventually awaken.
And their health and freedom will no longer be taken.

Printed in the United States
by Baker & Taylor Publisher Services